DATE DUE

AUG 10 1998			
SEP 18 1998			
NOV 13 1998			
MAY 28 1999			
AUG 22 1999			

THE GREAT KETTLES

A Tale of Time

WRITTEN AND ILLUSTRATED BY

DEAN MORRISSEY

HARRY N. ABRAMS, INC., PUBLISHERS

In memory of Dennis Morrissey and Gary Morrissey.

For my wife, Shan, without whom this book would not have been possible.

Special thanks to my mother, Mary.

*F*rom his bedroom window, Joey gazed out on his new neighborhood. It all looked strange, unfamiliar. He paced around his room, down the hall, back to the window. Everything felt wrong about this new house. The place smelled musty, the floors squeaked in the wrong places, he saw the wrong houses when he looked out of the window, the wrong trees. The tall grandfather clock echoed in the hallway. Worst of all, his friend Henry wasn't there. Henry was back where Joey belonged, in his old hometown.

Voices rising up the stairs in the half-empty house caught Joey's attention. He crept over to the bannister to listen. A woman from next door had come to welcome Joey's family to town.

"Professor Throttleman used to live in this house," the woman was saying to Joey's mother. "He was a scientist, an inventor. Most of his inventions were pretty farfetched. Used to see him wandering from room to room in his robe, wearing some sort of fantastic helmet. Some thought he was crazy, you know. The noises that used to come from the attic. We just never knew . . . we thought the house might just go up at any moment.

"Well, one night a strange sound came from the attic. The windows glowed bright as the sun. The noise grew louder and louder . . . and then . . . silence and darkness. And that was that. It's been forty years now. The house has been vacant ever since."

Joey's mind raced as he bounded up the stairs to the attic.

"I wonder what he left behind," Joey thought, "I wonder where he went."

As Joey entered the attic, he spotted a pile of clutter in a corner. One box caught his eye. It was an old wooden fruit crate with a brightly colored

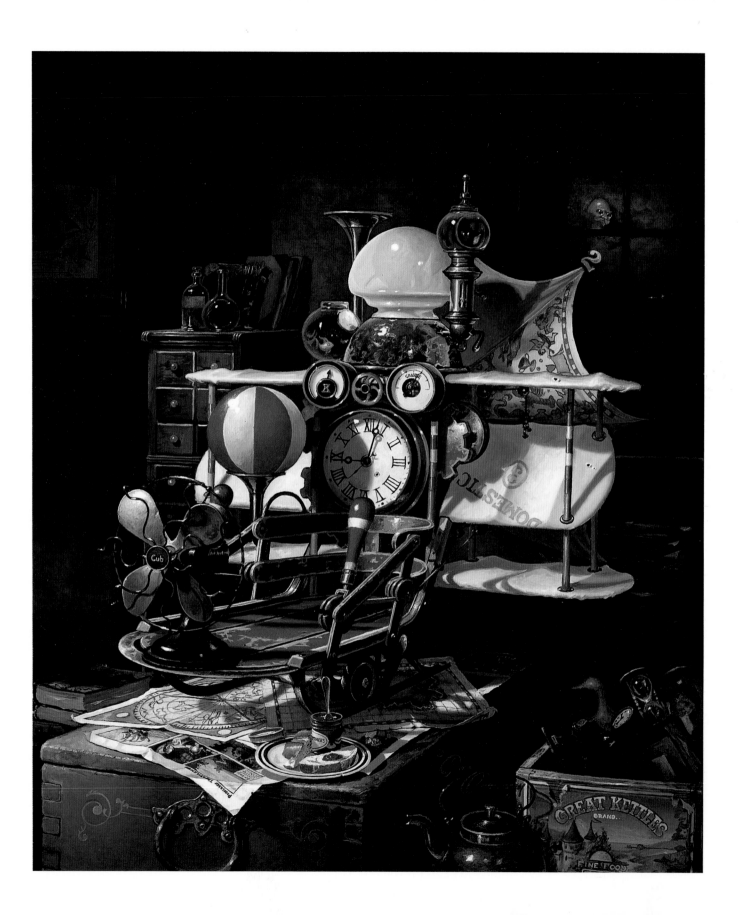

printed label showing a beautiful scene of a castle in a far-off land and the words "Great Kettles" in red and yellow letters.

In the crate Joey found some glass beakers and tubes and a dusty old book. The parched leather cover crackled as he slowly opened it. Inside were pages filled with words and sketches. Joey leafed through the book and stopped at a page marked with a red satin bookmark. It was a drawing of an old-fashioned sleigh fitted with gears, pipes, a propeller, and wings. Below it was written "Time Machine, by Prof. T. A. Throttleman." At the bottom of the page were some dates with notes.

"June 12: Still something not quite right. Won't start," one entry read.

"June 13: The machine will work. I'm sure of it. Tomorrow will test for time travel."

"June 14:"

Joey closed the book. "June 14 is blank," he exclaimed. "The professor vanished into time. Wow! If I could do that I could go and visit Henry whenever I wanted."

Joey set to work building a time machine using the professor's drawing. He gathered the parts from old things he found in the attic. A wooden sled took the place of the sleigh. An umbrella stood in for what Professor Throttleman had labeled the "time disk." On he went this way, fitting and matching, substituting and dreaming. He imagined himself riding the sled back to his old bedroom, or picking up Henry and going someplace far back in time.

Lost in his work, he didn't hear his mother come in from the second floor landing.

"What on earth are you building, Joey?"

"I'm making a time machine, Mom, so I can go back and visit Henry. Also, I think I might find Professor Throttleman."

"So you were eavesdropping this morning. Well, are you planning on leaving right away?"

"If it's okay with you."

"Just be back by dinnertime," she said. "Oh, and if you find the professor invite him to join us. I'll set an extra plate."

Finally, the sleigh looked complete. Joey climbed into the seat with the old book in front of him and leafed through it, looking for starting instructions. There weren't any, so he pulled a lever at random. Suddenly, the sled shuddered. Joey could feel his heart beating in his chest. The light atop the wings blinked on and the umbrella began to twirl, and then the whole machine shook and lifted off the floor. Joey dropped the book, and as he watched it fall it seemed to grow larger and larger. But it wasn't that. Joey and the sled were shrinking, and soon they were no bigger than a sparrow and were flying wildly around the attic.

The sled darted in between the rafters and across the room, then turned in a wide arc and plunged right at the "Great Kettles" crate.

Joey screamed and braced for the crash.

But he didn't crash. He flew right into the label.

A strong, fresh burst of ocean air hit Joey in the face and took his breath away. He was streaking across an open sky. His eyes watered as he looked around. Then, the light above the wings went out, and the sled spun over and over, toward the ground, where it landed with a crash.

When Joey came to he heard sea gulls and the lapping sound of water. He was lying on a beach. A few yards away the time machine was half-buried in a dune. One runner was bent and pieces of glass were broken and scattered on the sand. The umbrella was floating in the waves.

Joey stood up and scanned the horizon and spotted a tower in the distance. "Maybe there's somebody there who can give me some directions," he thought, and he began walking.

Midway along, a deep creaking sound filled the air. An enormous shadow rolled over him. Looking up, Joey was startled to see a wooden ship gliding through the air, carrying a great glass ball full of light. The ship touched down on the water and sailed in the direction of the tower.

Joey started for the tower, which was shaped like the big grandfather clock in his front hall. When he reached it, he found a door at the bottom. Joey knocked, and the door swung open. Inside was a winding circular staircase. He called out, "Anyone home?" and when no answer came, he started climbing the stairs.

When Joey reached the top he found himself inside a clockworks. Light streamed in through the glass clockface and glanced off the brass gears, shafts, and shuttles. But something was wrong. It was eerily still. The clock wasn't working.

Joey took another step into the room and saw an old man fast asleep in his chair, an open book on his lap. Joey froze.

The man was shifting in his chair, eyes still closed, smiling dreamily, when suddenly he sat up with a look of horror on his face.

"The clock has stopped," he bellowed. "Edmund, come at once!"

From a tiny door in the wall a rabbit appeared.

"Whatever is wrong, sir?"

"The clock, Edmund. It has stopped. That's what's wrong!"

The rabbit looked at his watch. "Oh dear, my watch has stopped, too. This can't be good."

"Good? Good? It's calamitous! When this clock stops, time itself stands still! There's only one thing that can stop this clock, Edmund. Do you know what that is?"

"A worn-out sprocket tooth, perhaps," offered the rabbit.

"No, Edmund," the old man snapped. "A time traveler. The clock sensed a time traveler and shut down. Someone has invaded the Great Kettles and we must find him at once!"

At that moment Joey was backing into the shadows to hide and his foot hit a chime. BONG!

The old man spun around. "What! What was that?" He peered into the shadows. "You there," he said, "come out into the light at once!"

Joey stepped forward.

"Now then, who are you and how did you get here?" The old man studied Joey, walking slowly around him.

"I'm Joey. I built a time machine using Professor Throttleman's plans and I found all of the parts. I just wanted to go back in time and visit my friend Henry. Do you know him?"

"Enough!" said the old man, waving his hand. "You've no idea what you've done."

"Absolutely no idea," Edmund chimed in.

"You are now standing in the middle of the Perpetual Absolute Standard Time Clock. And I am Father Time. Edmund is my assistant. We have been keeping time forever. The clock only shuts down when it senses someone traveling through time. Then everything stops so that no one can meddle with history. It's now my job to get the world started again.

"Come with me," the old man said. "And Edmund, I think now might be a good time to get out the oilcan and attend to these gears."

Father Time brought Joey to the other side of the tower.

"You've stumbled into a place called the Great Kettles. We lie just across the Sea of Time. These islands are home to the keepers of the Earth, the Sun, the Moon, and the Stars. Here we also generate the weather, move the tides, and cause the winds to blow—and, of course, keep time. At least we did until you came along," Father Time said, allowing himself a little smile.

"Look there. The Man in the Moon has come in to dock. The Keeper of the Light, who carries the Sun across the sky, is in port. The Sandman is flying home as well."

"The Sandman?" Joey asked brightly. "Oh, I know him."

Father Time wasn't listening. "Without time," he continued, "there's nothing for them to do. I'm sure they'll all be grateful for a little rest. But now we have to think about getting you back home."

"Can you do it?" asked Joey.

"Can I?" replied Father Time. "I've got to. I've got to."

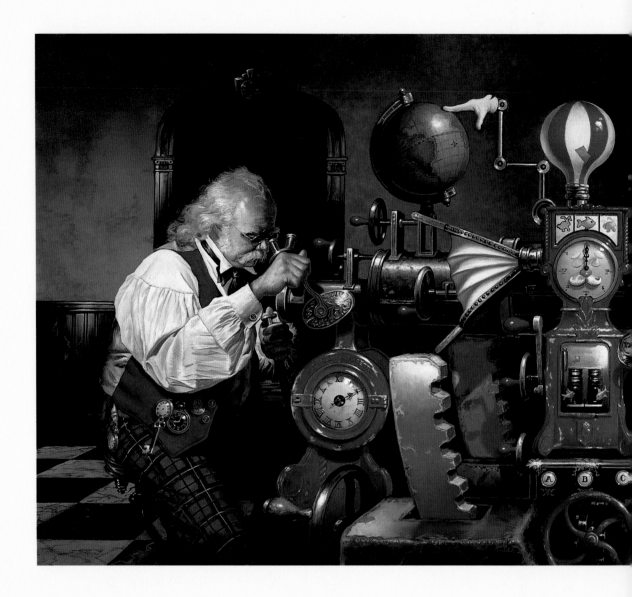

"Couldn't we just fix my time machine? I could go home in that," said Joey.

"Ha! That bucket of bolts," snorted Father Time. "It won't operate in this dimension. That's why it shut down, and that's why we shut down. We can't have time travelers crossing the Sea of Time and mucking around with history. Follow me!"

Joey followed Father Time into another room of the tower where there was a fantastic machine shaped like a cannon. Father Time positioned Joey at one end and aimed the machine.

"Don't be afraid, Joey. This is a Centurioscope, a telescope of time."

Gears whirred and shafts creaked. Joey stood completely still. He could see nothing inside

the end of the scope, but he sensed it moving, like the X-ray machine at the dentist.

"First it will read you," Father Time said. "And then it will search through time and tell me exactly where you left from. Aha, yes. Come, take a look."

Joey walked around the machine and squinted into the eyepiece. He saw himself sitting in the sled in his attic.

"Hey, that's me!"

"Good. Now, let's read these gauges and we'll know just where to go. Edmund!" the old man shouted out. "Time maps, please. And get the ship ready."

Perched on the roof of the tower was a great winged ship. Father Time climbed in first and Joey sat beside him.

Father Time looked perplexed by all the controls in front of him, and several times turned off switches that he had just turned on.

"Oh dear, it's been so long," he was saying under his breath as he shifted levers and pulled on knobs.

Finally, the machine coughed to life.

"Hang on, Joey."

But there was practically nothing to hang on to. First the ship climbed like a rocket and then began to swoop and plunge. Father Time fought to control it. Just as they were skimming over the ground the ship bucked and twisted and Joey fell off the side.

"Oh dear oh dear oh dear," Father Time cried. "What have I done?"

Joey landed on the crest of a grassy hill and tumbled down the bank. He came to rest unhurt beside a dirt road. In the distance was the clock tower.

"Here we go again," Joey said to himself as he started walking.

Soon he heard the clip-clopping of a horse and buggy. He turned around to see what it was when a familiar voice cried out, "Joey, is that you? Off on another adventure?"

It was the Sandman, an old acquaintance.

"Climb aboard, lad, and meet my friend the Man in the Moon."

"Hello," Joey said. "I've seen you many times. It's a pleasure to meet you."

"Humph," replied the Moon. "Wish I could say the same."

"Pay no attention to the old grouch, Joey," the Sandman said. "He's quite pleased to have a rest. He's been floating around in the sky so long he's forgotten how to behave around people."

The Man in the Moon hunched down and grumbled.

"I was on my way home with Father Time, and suddenly I'm back here again. I've got to find him."

"Well, here we are in the village already. And there's your Father Time!"

Father Time came rushing up. "Joey!" he said, out of breath. "Thank heaven you're all right. Sandman, Moon, how are you?"

"I couldn't be better. Don't ask Moon," the Sandman said.

Father Time nodded politely, but said, "Joey, come along. There's someone we must meet at once."

Joey said goodbye and climbed out of the checkered cab.

Joey followed Father Time through the village and down a winding road until they came to a cottage. They went in without knocking and found themselves in the middle of a laboratory crowded with glass beakers, machine parts, and piles of hardware. A man sat in the midst of the clutter wearing a funny-looking helmet.

"Professor, I must speak with you at once," said Father Time.

The man held up his hand for silence, then frowned, sighed, shook his head, let out a laugh, and said "Yes, of course!" And as he spoke, a light at the top of the helmet lit up. The man took off the helmet and stood up.

"We shall need a Time Elevator! To return to his own time, the boy must travel vertically," he said emphatically.

"Yes, vertically," Father Time nodded, "but how did you know of Joey's problem?"

"The Kettles is a very small place. Joey, I'm Professor Throttleman. The talk in the village is that you built a time machine."

"*Your* time machine, I think, Professor Throttleman. I used your plans. I live in your old house."

"That's what I suspected. I've often wondered what happened to my house and everything left in the attic. But my design was flawed. I planned to fly through history, and I never got past the Great Kettles. My ship crashed, but the clock never stopped. I guess this is where I was meant to be. So now, to start the P.A.S.T. clock we've got to get you back where you belong."

"Now then," Professor Throttleman said. And he walked to an old oak drafting table, took a pencil from behind his ear, and began drawing plans.

"We'll build it in the pendulum chamber of the clock tower," he said as he drew. "Can we count on Edmund's help, Father Time?"

"I'll vouch for Edmund," Father Time said.

As the Professor continued sketching and making notes, Joey recognized the handwriting from the old book in his attic.

Finally, the Professor put his pencil down.

"We'll build the machine, Joey. But there's something that you need to do. For this machine to get you through time, you will need a special light, one that travels faster than light itself and can reveal the future."

The Professor walked over to a map on the wall.

"This is a map of the Great Kettles. Mother Nature lives here, on Copper Kettle Island. Seek her out and ask for her help. She's very wise. She can be hard to find, but listen to the wind and you'll be all right. Now then, off you go. Father Time will take you to the train. When you have the special light come back to the clock tower. We'll be waiting."

Clacking and chugging, the train wheezed its way to a stop.

"Looks like the Cow That Jumped Over the Moon is the only other passenger today," Father Time said.

A single door opened and Joey climbed aboard.

Father Time waved his arm and the train lurched and pulled out of the station.

"Once you have the light," Father Time called out, "the train will bring you back."

Almost before he knew it, the train had crossed a bridge and pulled into the station on Copper Kettle Island. Joey stepped out onto a cobblestone street, whose stones soon gave way to a grassy path. He looked around in all directions with no idea where to begin his search. Then, he heard a whispering in the trees ahead and walked on.

It was sunny and warm as Joey walked along the path. He passed an open meadow that was like the field behind Henry's house, where they used to meet and have adventures. As Joey walked on his spirits sank. Would he ever get back home? Even going back to the new house would be great. At least Henry could come over sometimes.

Joey felt a little tickle of wind playing around his legs and slowly climbing higher and higher up his body. It was the oddest thing, to feel the wind like this, but then something even odder happened. The wind circled around his head and in a soft, whispery voice began to speak.

"Thissss way," it said slowly, over and over, "thissss way. If it's Mother Nature you seek, come thissss way."

The wind pushed him along the path and then onto the bank of a clear, still river. There, gliding toward him was a beautiful woman in an elegant boat trailing flowers. Animals of all kinds crowded the banks to get a glimpse of her. As she drew near, the wind died down, and the boat stopped in midstream. Mother Nature lifted her outstretched hand toward Joey.

"Time is as vital as the air," she said, in the same whispery voice as the wind. "The right path is never clear, but the journey is always a journey forward, never back. Go home, dear boy. This light will help you find your way."

A fairy no bigger than a hummingbird flew up from Mother Nature's hand and brought Joey a tiny lantern. It glowed brightly. Then, a gentle breeze came up and the boat slipped downstream.

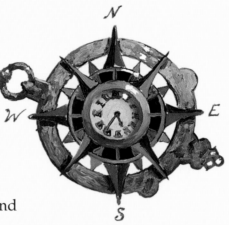

Joey barely remembered the trip back to the clock tower. Edmund met him at the train station and walked him back to the tower. Inside, in the high chamber, a huge and elaborate machine hung from cables and pulleys.

Joey was astounded. "How did Professor Throttleman build this so fast?"

"We don't live by measured time here, Joey," Father Time explained. He was standing in the control chamber of the Time Elevator.

"Did you find the light?" the Professor asked.

Joey held up the tiny lantern.

"Splendid!" said the Professor. "Now, Joey, I must warn you. The Time Elevator is an unpredictable machine despite our best calculations and efforts. If something goes wrong you could end up back among the dinosaurs or as a stableboy for the Knights of the Round Table. Once you land back in real time, the clock starts, and that's that. I want you to know, Joey, that you are welcome to stay here with us. We'd take good care of you. It's up to you. What do you think?"

Joey thought for a moment. "I want to go home."

"You're a brave boy. What are we waiting for? Let's try it!" the Professor cheered.

Using a rope and pulley they hoisted Joey up into the Time Elevator.

"Do you see the lever marked Retro, Joey?"

"I see it, Professor."

"Put your hand on the Retro lever and never take it off, no matter what. When the Elevator stops you'll have about five seconds to see if you're in the right place—on the sled in your attic, where your journey began. If you land anywhere else—and I mean *anywhere* else—pull the lever. You'll be returned to the clock tower and we can make the necessary adjustments."

"Ready, Joey? Remember. On the sled. In your attic. If you're not there and the clock starts, you're stuck."

The Elevator slowly lifted into the chamber. Joey shut his eyes and struggled to keep his hand on the Retro lever as the machine shook and rocked through Time. The noise of gears grinding and clocks ticking was deafening. Bursts of colorful lights flashed past. Suddenly all light and sound stopped.

Joey opened his eyes. He found himself sitting in an old rusted car in a garage. He looked out through the windshield and saw his house. The car had been in the garage when they had moved in.

"Wow! I'm home," Joey yelled. And he reached for the door handle to jump out of the car.

Then he remembered the Professor's instructions.

"Wait a second," Joey said. "I was supposed to land in the attic, on the sled. I have to go back! Where's the Retro lever?"

"Retro . . . Retro," he said, searching the car. Then he saw the gear shifter: "1, 2, 3, R," it read. He pushed the stiff old lever into "R" and went whizzing back through the dark void.

The trip back was longer and rougher. When Joey returned to the clock tower he was so exhausted he could barely open his eyes. The Professor and Father Time helped him to his feet in the control chamber of the Time Elevator.

"I was so close!" said Joey. "I landed in the garage, in the old car."

"Not close enough," replied the Professor.

Father Time held up the lantern. "You forgot something, Joey. I'm surprised you got as close as you did without it. In the excitement you must have left it behind."

"Are you up for another try?" asked the Professor as he adjusted the settings.

"Yes," said Joey, "and, by the way, my mother said to invite you for dinner if I found you. You could even come back and live with us in your old house."

"Tell your mom thanks," replied the Professor, "but I've got a lot of work to do. Besides, that house is your place now. I belong here."

They all said goodbye and the Elevator was off again. When the humming and flashing and whizzing through the dark stopped, Joey found himself sitting on the sled in his attic. He looked around just to be sure before he took his hand off the Retro lever.

"I'm back!" he yelled happily.

It was as if he had never left the room. He got off the sled and saw the Great Kettles crate, the beakers, the Professor's old book on the floor. Had he really gone? Then he noticed the little light burning at his feet. It was the lantern. The lantern!

"Joey," his mother called from the bottom of the attic stairs.

"Yes, Mom?"

"Clean up for dinner. Henry's mother just called. She's bringing him over for the weekend."

"Henry! All right! I'll be right down." He scooped up the lantern and the old book. "Wait till I tell him about this!"

"Did you ever find the Professor in your travels, Joey?" his mother asked. "Is he coming for dinner?"

"I found him, Mom. He said thanks, but he's pretty busy right now."

"Okay," she replied. "Another time then."

INDEX OF PAINTINGS

EDITOR: Robert Morton

DESIGNER: Darilyn Lowe Carnes

Library of Congress Cataloging-in-Publication Data

Morrissey, Dean.

The Great Kettles: a tale of time/by Dean Morrissey.

p. cm.

Summary: Hoping to visit the friend he had to leave behind when his family moved, Joey builds a time machine and makes an eventful trip to the land where Father Time, Mother Nature, the Man in the Moon, and other such characters live.

ISBN 0–8109–3396–9 (hardcover)

[1. Time travel—Fiction. 2. Moving, Household—Fiction.]

I. Title.

PZ7. M84532Gr 1997

[Fic]—dc21 97–5749

First Edition

Printed and bound in Hong Kong

Harry N. Abrams, Inc.

100 Fifth Avenue

New York, N.Y. 10011

www.abramsbooks.com